The Case of
The Missing Tooth Fairy

By: Joleen Michellie

The Case of
The Missing Tooth Fairy

By: Joleen Michellie

Written and Illustrated by: Joleen Michellie
Cover Art by: Kaylee Mary

Published by: JoBooks 2023

ISBN: 978-0-9908502-2-9

Library of Congress Control Number: 2023904835

Table of Contents

Dedication & Preface

Glossary

Dedication:

This book is dedicated to my late grandmother: Betty Ann, for the countless memories made in her kitchen, the endless hours spent watching rainbows dance throughout the beautiful home she and my grandfather Bill shared, (courtesy of their crystal sun catchers) and for their always ready, always pristine guestroom, which is now perfectly preserved in chapter two of this very book. (Although I did leave out the many model cars and family pictures of my grandfathers that were in there. I'll have to save those for another book.) Thank you, grandma, for sharing your love for reading and writing with me. For forcing me to practice typing, even when I didn't want to. I now have your touch lamp on the nightstand in my bedroom, and your ballerina pictures hanging on the wall of an ever-ready guestroom in my own house.

Also, to my mother, Kathleen: who is known as "Nana" to my own children, your world famous banana bread is nothing short of inspirational.

Lastly, but certainly not least, to my amazing kids: you are always a source for great writing material, and I love each of you endlessly. I know of more than one occasion, where my own children have been left to ponder: The Case of the Missing Tooth Fairy.

Preface:

This book is best enjoyed being read to you by a loved one, over thick slices of banana bread, served with ice cold milk, and of course, some perfectly popped popcorn too. Cinnamon rolls with bacon, or pizza and chips are also highly enjoyable while reading this book.

Chapter 1

The Lost Tooth

Annabelle MacShannon stared out the window of the school bus. She was wiggling her tooth, when suddenly, BUMP!

"Ouch," she thought, as she looked down seeing something hard and white in her bloody fingers. A huge smile burst onto her face. She'd lost her tooth!

Turning to tell a friend, she looked at the empty seat across from her. Her excitement faded, as she remembered they'd already gotten off.

Her sister sat too many rows up ahead. She couldn't have gotten her attention, at least not without getting into trouble. It was almost their stop anyways. Carefully, she tucked her tooth into her pocket, as the bus came to a stop.

Annabelle stepped off the school bus and hurried to catch up with her older sister; pulling her tooth from her pocket. "Marysue, Marysue, look, I lost my tooth!"

"Cool, don't drop it, or you won't get any money from the tooth fairy." Her older sister warned. Annabelle stopped to tuck her tooth safely away.

Marysue kept walking. Annabelle hurried again to catch up. The girls walked along the sidewalk, under constant shade from the trees that lined their street.

There was a large oak that marked the corner of their property. At the base of the tree a large crack, that buckled the sidewalk, came into view. Their eyes met with anticipation.

Both girls began walking faster. Gripping their backpacks tighter, as their deliberately long strides broke into a full out run.

They laughed as they raced each other the rest of the way home. Neither of them slowed along their rose bush lined, white picket fence.

"Beat you!" Marysue exclaimed, as she dropped the red flag on their standard, black mailbox. She reached inside to retrieve the mail.

Annabelle had stopped just short of the finish line though. She was holding her arm. "What happened?" Marysue asked apologetically. "Rose thorn got me." Annabelle sniveled.

The red front door of their white house burst open, "Girls, hurry in. Come on now, we've got to clean you up and get going!" Their mother called urgently. She waved them inside peering up and down the street.

"Probably checking to see if any of the neighbors had seen her in her robe with her hair wrapped up in a towel." Annabelle thought. The girls hurried up the brick steps and into their house.

"Oh, just look at the two of you." Mrs. MacShannon said franticly, "Go and get yourselves cleaned up."

It was clear to Annabelle that her mother was in quite a hurry.

Their flower print duffle bags were already packed. They sat side by side, embroidered names facing outward, on top of the cedar bench in the entry way. The girls were going to their grand-mother's house.

Their mother would be attending a fancy awards banquet that night, with their father, Mr. MacShannon.

Annabelle didn't know why Mom seemed to be so nervous,

Dad was the one accepting the award.

"Mom, I need a Band-Aid." She demanded as she was being ushered down the hall towards her bedroom.

Her mother took her hand away, "That is quite the scratch you've got there young lady, but I'm afraid I don't have a Band-Aid big enough for that. Clean it up good with lots of soap while you're in the shower."

"Shower! Don't I get a bath?" Annabelle much preferred having a bath to taking showers.

"No time for a bath! Shower, and make it quick!"

It didn't seem she'd been in the shower long, when her mother poked her head into the bathroom. "Annabelle, you get dried off and dressed right now! Your sister's already waiting, ready by the door."

She peered out from behind the curtain, shampoo suds so thick they were hiding the redness of her hair.

"I mean it young lady. Out now, get that rinsed off!" Annabelle's mother came in and scooped up her clothes off the floor, tossing them into the dirty clothes basket.

"Hurry up Anna! I'm starting the car."

Annabelle went as quickly as she could. When she reached the front door, her mother was there waiting for her. The bags and her sister were already loaded into the idling car.

Chapter 2

Nana's House

The drive to Nana's house was always pleasant with the winding roads up through all the farms and pastures. There were lots of things to look at out the windows.

Pulling into Nana's long dusty driveway, all of the MacShannon girls were excited, even mom.

The dogs leapt from the front porch, running to greet them halfway, as they looped around the large willow tree. Nana stood from her rocking chair and made her way down the porch steps.

"Oh, my girls, my girls!" Nana said as she held her hands wide, competing with the dogs for her hugs.

Annabelle showed off her scratch, and Nana covered it in her famous 'all better kisses'.

"Thank you so much for this." Mom said, as she handed off the overnight bags.

"Oh, it's no trouble at all Dear. You two go and enjoy your evening. Girls, hug your ma'ma so she can get going now."

They said their goodbyes and stood on the porch waving to mom as she drove out of sight.

"Oooooooo, I'm so excited to have you two all to myself. Let's get you all settled in."

Nana ushered the girls inside. The smell of fresh baked banana bread filled their noses. They didn't linger very long in the entry way.

The walls were filled with display cases of small collector's spoons and shelves of several teacup collections. Porcelain dolls and glass candy dishes were neatly arranged on the tops of Nana's dark cherry wood furniture.

The girls were careful not to knock into anything as they walked by with their bags. As they turned the corner, collages of family photos, new and old, lined the hallway.

In the guest bedroom, things looked exactly as the girls expected. A faint smell of moth balls floated in the air, as they entered the familiar room. Everything was in its proper place.

There were two, meticulously made, twin sized beds with dark cherry headboards. A large, flat Raggedy Ann doll, with bright red yarn for hair, was perched at the head of one bed. The matching Raggedy Andy doll was on the other.

Pillows were tucked in tightly by the white woven, textured blankets with tassels hanging off the end corners.

Each bed was positioned on opposite walls. A nightstand, with a brass touch lamp on it, sat between the two.

Above the headboards hung three majestic paintings of ballerinas. They looked as if they could dance right out of their matching wooden picture frames.

Marysue plopped down onto the bed, near the window, moving aside the oversized Raggedy Ann doll. She began tapping out a rhythm on the touch lamp, which sat on an heirloom doily. With each touch, the lamp shone brighter, until the fourth touch turned the lamp off. Marysue continued tapping.

Annabelle set down her duffle bag and was immediately drawn to the dollhouse in the corner.

Nana sat on the end of the bed, near the doll house and asked "So, how was school today? I want to hear all about it."

Before Annabelle could think to answer...

"I had a spelling test today." Marysue stated, still tapping at the lamp.

Then, suddenly, eyes wide, a look of absolute horror swept over Annabelle, as she shrieked, "My TOOTH! Oh no, oh no, oh no!"

Nana reached down to comfort her, "Your tooth?" She asked softly.

"I lost my tooth, on the school bus today, I— I put it in my pocket." Annabelle's hands shot down to her sides, but these weren't the same pockets. "Oh, Nana, I lost my tooth!"

Nana hugged her as she began to cry.

Marysue stopped her tapping on the lamp, "It's probably still in your pocket Anna, don't worry. Mom was in such a hurry today— I doubt she started the laundry."

Sobs continued, "But you said if I lost my tooth that the Tooth Fairy wouldn't come, and now, I— I lost it."

Marysue came and put a hand on her little sister's shoulder, "It'll be ok— Hey, I bet there's banana bread in the kitchen?"

Marysue looked with questioning eyes to Nana who smiled back at her.

"Well, there sure is. Fresh baked this morning specially for you two." Nana stood up slapping her knees.

"Come on girls, I'll cut you up a slice, and Anna dear, don't worry. Tooth fairies are smart as they come. Your tooth won't be lost for long. Come to the kitchen with me, and I'll tell you all I know about tooth fairies."

Marysue took off down the hall, sliding on the dark wooden floor in her socks. Annabelle got up, wiped the tears from her cheeks, and followed her nose toward the warm kitchen.

Chapter 3

Fairy Tales

Nana's kitchen was nothing short of magical. Countless memories were made there: Memories of baking cookies, of being Nana's official taste testers, and of Nana's story telling.

Rainbows shone in every direction. Light from the setting sun, refracted off the dazzling crystal sun-catcher that dangled in the window, above the kitchen sink.

Annabelle climbed up onto a stool next to her sister. Nana reached into the cupboard above the breakfast bar where they sat.

"Nothing but the best for my girls." She said, setting the blue and white, antique saucers onto the tile countertop.

Nana placed a generous slice of her world famous banana bread on each plate and served it up with an ice-cold glass of milk. A glass, glass!

At home they always used plastic cups, just in case. But at Nana's, it was nothing but the best.

Annabelle was dipping her bread into her milk when, PLOP, a chunk fell off and milk splashed out of her glass.

Maryann giggled.

Before Annabelle had time to fret, Nana was there with cloth in hand. She wiped up the milk splashes and handed Anna a spoon, winking with a smile.

"Nana," Annabelle said through a mouth full of soggy banana bread "Tell us what you know about the Tooth Fairy."

"Oh, yes, of course," Nana said as she rinsed out the cloth, "well— let's see. Where to start? Did you know that fairies are just three inches tall?"

She wrung out the cloth, hanging it over the faucet, peering out her window deep in thought, "and…" she paused for a moment. "Well, the tooth fairies have one of the most important— most special jobs in the whole fairy community. Only tooth fairies are trusted with direct human contact! All the fairies have their different jobs you know."

"Jobs?" Annabelle asked.

"Yes, jobs. Some fairies look after injured little bugs," Nana pinched her fingers together to show how small "or there's the ones who help our snow to melt and our plants to grow," she gestured to her windowsill of various pots of cacti and succulents. "Some collect food with the bees, and others collect wish-coins from the wishing wells."

"But Nana, you can't take the wish-coins, or those wishes won't come true!" Marysue chimed in.

Nana reached across the counter placing her hand on Marysue's shoulder, "Oh, no my dear. You cannot take the wish-coins, but fairies are the ones who gather the coins to help grant those wishes My Sweet. Their job is very important too. They have to be very careful which wish-coins they collect. You both know of course a wish doesn't come true if you blab about it. So, they won't choose a coin if the wisher has told their wish out loud, and of course, the wish must have been made with pureness of heart too.

Yes the fairies are very selective on which wishes they choose; otherwise there would be no coins left in the fountains and wells. Once wishes are chosen, and retrieved, the wishing well fairies take the wish-coins and add them to the great Waiting Wishes Wall." Nana went on, "The Waiting Wishes Wall is entirely made up of wish-coins, and it's so long that it lines the whole northern border of their city."

The girls looked stunned.

Nana was going about cleaning up the kitchen. As she put away the bread and was cleaning up the dishes, she noticed their shocked faces. She smiled and continued, "Well, wherever do you suppose they get all that money to give out to all the kids in all the world who lose their teeth? I mean honestly girls! It's not like fairies can just get a regular old job and work at the market— and they would never steal money from a bank. Fairies are far too kind and good to do a thing like that. No, no, the very coins you get under your pillows from the tooth fairy are the cherished wishes, once cast into the water with high hopes of that wish coming true. Then the tooth fairy comes to place those wish-coins under your pillow, and as you dream, you help those wishes to come true."

Annabelle tilted her head thoughtfully. "How do my dreams help?" She asked.

"Because dream dust is magic." Nana stated plainly. "Should I pop us some popcorn for our movie tonight?"

The girls nodded excitedly both exclaiming together "yes, please!"

Then Marysue cleared her throat, "So, let me see if I've got this all straight. There are lots more fairies out there than just the Tooth Fairy. They all have jobs. One of those jobs is to go get the wish-coins and stack those on some wall someplace. Then the tooth fairies take those coins, and that's what they put under all our pillows?"

11

Marysue continued "So when I wake up from dreaming with wish-coins under my pillow then, someone else's wish came true?"

"Well, not exactly. Wish granting is quite complex. There's a lot more to it. Once your dream dust is on those coins, it depends on what happens to them next. Something needs to light the magic."

"Light the magic?" both girls asked. "Yes, well see, magic can be lost or it can be ignited." Nana put the first popcorn bag into the microwave, the BEEP BEEP BEEP of the buttons was clear, but the hum of the microwave was soon muffled by questions from the girls.

"How can magic be lost?" Marysue asked.

"What's ignited?" Annabelle asked at the same time, her words crowding in on top of Marysue's question.

Nana smiled patiently, "To ignite is what happens when you start a fire. Something must happen to start that magic dust up — but, something could also happen to knock all that magic dust right off of there. It all depends on where those coins end up next. You could spend them at a store, they'll still have their magic dust — but, just spending the coin on something ordinary won't ignite it. The magic will still be with that coin and that wish will still have an opportunity to come true. You could lose it, and again, that lost coin will still hold its magic and the opportunity for a granted wish. If something bad happens to the coins, it'll knock that magic dust right off."

"Bad like what?" Marysue asked.

"Oh, I don't know. I suppose if a boy went to school with tooth fairy money to buy himself a milk, and then someone took that money away from him, that would surely be enough to snuff out the magic."

"I still don't get it." Said Marysue. Annabelle nodded in agreement.

POP, POP, the popcorn started, POP, POP, POP, POP…

"Come grab your bowls." Nana said.

The girls hopped off their barstools and walked around the counter into the kitchen. Marysue opened a bottom cupboard where all the large mixing bowls were stored.

"I want the purple one!" Annabelle said in a hurry.

"Which one do you want Nana?" asked Marysue.

"You pick for me," Nana said. She was standing at the microwave waiting patiently. Her thumb resting over the 'end' button, as she was listening to hear when the slowing of the pops was just right to stop.

"You get the flower one then, and the red and white one's for me." Marysue said, placing three large bowls onto the counter.

"I want that one!" Annabelle blurted out, reaching for the theater style square bowl with red and white stripes.

"Now, Annabelle, you got to choose first."

Annabelle crossed her arms in a pout.

"Annabelle—" Nana's voice had a tone of warning, "The purple one will do just fine. It's attitudes like this that make those precious wish-coins lose all their magic."

Nana stopped the microwave with 14 seconds left to go. The bag steamed as she tore open the top, a smell of butter poured out around them. Nana dumped out the entire bag into the floral bowl, leaving the girls' bowls empty.

This was odd, she'd always served up each of the popcorn bags evenly into each of their bowls.

She turned to put another bag into the microwave, BEEP, BEEP, BEEP.

"I think I'll try explaining this concept using popcorn. Nana reached into her bowl pulling out a single plump kernel flake.

The girls could feel their mouths watering. Annabelle actually licked her lips. Their eyes were fixed on that single piece of popcorn Nana held up on display in her finger tips.

"Let's pretend that you both have some money." Nana reached into her glass dish of mixed nuts and placed some in front of each girl.

"Here's your money, and here's yours. Ok, so who wants to buy some popcorn?"

The girls smiled raising their hands high into the air.

"Great, well I have popcorn to sell, but we're going to pretend that it's not just any old popcorn, it's magic wishing popcorn!" Excitement sparkled in their eyes as they listened intently, their mouths still watering, aching for a taste of the popcorn they could smell so strongly.

"So, Marysue, you'll go first. You can buy this first piece of popcorn for 1 nut."

Marysue slid over a nut, Nana handed her the piece of popcorn. Marysue popped the popcorn into her mouth and made a satisfying crunch.

"Your turn Annabelle, I will sell you this second piece of popcorn for 2 nuts."

Annabelle slid over the 2 nuts and got her 1 piece of popcorn.

"Now then, if we're pretending those are wishing popcorns, do you think either of those wishes came true?"

The girls didn't answer. They honestly didn't know.

"Think about it, did anything special seem to happen to light up that magic?"

Still no answers.

"Let's keep going, this third piece of popcorn is going to cost you three nuts." Marysue paid the three nuts.

Nana continued onto Annabelle "This fourth piece of popcorn will cost you…"

"four nuts" the girls said.

They kept trading in turns five nuts, for the fifth piece, six nuts for the sixth piece, but when it came to the seventh piece of popcorn, Marysue didn't have enough nuts.

"I only have four left." She said.

Nana looked to Annabelle. "How about you, would you like to buy this seventh piece of popcorn?"

Annabelle looked down at her three nuts, then over to Marysue, and then her gaze fell onto the bowl of nuts.

"Ah, ah, ah, those are mine and not yours." Nana cautioned. And then it happened…

"Here, you can have mine." Marysue said, as she slid her last four nuts over to Annabelle. Suddenly she smiled.

Annabelle now had just enough for that seventh piece of popcorn.

Just then the explosion of POP, POP, POP, POP, POPs came from the microwave.

Nana stood laughing "You did it, you got it, and that my girls, is how you light the magic!" she exclaimed.

Annabelle still held a questioning look on her face, but Marysue smiled nodding.

"Could you feel the magic Mary?" Nana asked.

Marysue's smile grew. "Yeah!"

"How'd it feel?"

"It felt warm, felt good. Like even though I was giving away the last of my nuts, it was going to help Annabelle and that made me happy."

"You nailed it!" Nana said beaming with pride, she stood once again waiting by the microwave to stop it at just the right moment. When she pulled out the bag, she held it high up in the air and then dumped it all into Marysue's bowl saying, "And this is what the magic does after it's lit, right here, it just pours out on you."

The girls giggled as the popcorn fell, not all of it landing right into her bowl, as some of it bounced onto the counter top.

Annabelle's bowl was still empty though.

Marysue began picking up the extra pieces on the counter and putting them into her bowl. Then she dumped half of her popcorn into the empty purple bowl for Annabelle.

"Oooo, there you go, lighting up that magic again!" Nana said as she put the third bag of popcorn into the microwave.

"So, Nana, if you do nice things with the money you get from the tooth fairy, then that's what makes the magic start working?" Marysue asked.

"That's the golden ticket right there, charity never fails girls. To give with a grateful heart is the best gift you can give, not just to others, but to yourself."

They all dug into their popcorn as they waited for the last bag to finish.

Nana divided it equally between the girls. Then, they made their way to the living room to enjoy movie night, cuddled up with Nana under the covers, munching on their near perfect popcorn.

Chapter 4

A Very Busy Day

-Saturday-

Annabelle woke up to the sound of muffled voices and laughter. Someone was in the kitchen with Nana. She took in a sharp breath of excitement as she realized who it was, Mom and Dad!

The bed across the room was already empty. She wiped the sleep from her eyes, and headed down the hall, towards mixed smells of cinnamon rolls and the bacon she could now hear sizzling on the stove top.

"Well good morning sleepy head!" said Dad, interrupting his own story from the night before as he scooped Annabelle into his arms.

Marysue stood next to mom, a half-eaten cinnamon roll on the plate in front of her as she munched on a piece of bacon.

Nana saw Annabelle staring towards her sister. "You hungry" Nana asked, handing Annabelle her own plate.

Dad went back to telling about the awards ceremony: his speech, and of how he'd caught a lady who'd tripped and nearly fell off the stage in front of everyone.

Mom told of the fancy dresses, wonderful food, and the strong cocktails that gave her today's headache.

Annabelle had gobbled up her breakfast, which was good because in no time at all, they were leaving Nana's house. They had a busy day today. Marysue had the lead in the church play tomorrow and the dress rehearsal was tonight!

Everyone hugged their goodbyes as dad loaded the girls' bags into the car.

They all waved at Nana, who stood on the porch and the dogs chased after the car, barking their goodbyes down the gravel driveway. They ran back to Nana's porch as the MacShannon family turned onto the street.

Annabelle watched as the house disappeared from view. Meanwhile Mom and Marysue were going over the long list of everything they needed to get done for tonight's rehearsal.

It was decided that since Mom wasn't finished making alterations for the costumes, Dad would take Annabelle with him to pick up the pizza order, while Marysue practiced her lines on stage.

Of course, eating pizza wouldn't happen until after everyone helped make the stage props.

"Good thing Nana fed us breakfast, it's going to be a long day." Dad said.

As they pulled up to the church everyone was rushing around putting the final touches on each of the backdrops and making sure the props got into the right boxes.

Annabelle was busy painting a white cardboard fence. It reminded her of the fence at home. She wondered if there was any red paint so she could paint roses on there and make it just like the one at home.

Mom was busy measuring a boy in a tree costume that hung loosely on him.

Marysue was in the corner with a friend going over lines. Dad was up on stage hammering a wooden moon onto a backdrop of a city scape.

Annabelle walked all over the auditorium before finding the supply cabinet, and there in front of her were all the colors of paint she could dream of.

She was only looking for red, but heck, looking at all of these options, it was hard to choose just one shade. So she filled her arms with as much as she could carry and got back to work on painting the fence.

Everyone was working hard finishing their tasks, the dress rehearsal would be starting soon, when Marysue let out a cry "Oh Annabelle! What have you done! MOM! DAD! MOOOOOM!!!"

Both Dad and Mom rushed over. Dad was doing his best to hide a smirk.

"Oh, Annabelle." Said Mom.

"What?" Annabelle asked.

"You ruined it! That's what!" Marysue exclaimed.

Annabelle felt hurt, "What do you mean I ruined it? It's not ruined, you're ruined."

"Now girls." Dad intervened, "Honey, why don't you stay and, uh, well fix this. It's about time I go get all those pizzas anyway."

"Yes, that sounds like a very good idea." Mom and Dad kissed goodbye as Mom handed dad the keys.

"Come on Annabelle, I'm going to need your help carrying all those pizzas." Dad and Annabelle left the church and headed to the pizza place.

Mom stayed and got to work repainting the fence with Marysue.

Dad placed the pizza order, and they said it would be a 45 minute wait.

So, Dad and Annabelle went to the store to buy all kinds of other things they needed for the rehearsal dinner.

When they got back to the pizza place, the order wasn't quite ready yet. Dad and Annabelle played video games in pizza arcade while they waited.

Annabelle was thrilled to get away from all the craziness for a bit. It seemed like dad was glad for the break too.

"Order up, 15 extra large pizza's for MacShannon." the worker called out.

Annabelle helped hold open the door 'cause the stack of pizzas dad was carrying went clear past his head!

The back windows steamed up from the heat, and those pizzas smelled so good.

Annabelle wanted to eat a slice right away, but she knew better than to ask for one. It was for everybody, so she had to wait.

Back at the church helpers came to unload the drinks, chips, cookies, veggies, cups, plates, napkins, and pizzas.

The cast and crew all enjoyed a well earned meal before the dress rehearsal started.

Annabelle was excited to watch, but she fell asleep half way through. Dad had carried her to the car.

When they all got home, it was way past bedtime.

"Brush your teeth, then off to bed with you. We'll shower in the morning." Mom had said.

The girls were so tired they didn't even want to brush their teeth, but they did.

Mom and Dad tucked them into their beds and went down

the hall to put themselves to bed too. It had been a long day for everyone.

Just as Annabelle was about to drift back into sleep she remembered... her tooth!

She snuck out of bed, tiptoed back into the bathroom, and dug into the laundry bin. Looking for her pants… she found them! *"Oh please, please, please."* She thought, reaching into her pocket. There inside she felt, yes, it was her tooth. She kissed it, she was so happy. She sprinted back into bed and placed her tooth carefully under the pillow.

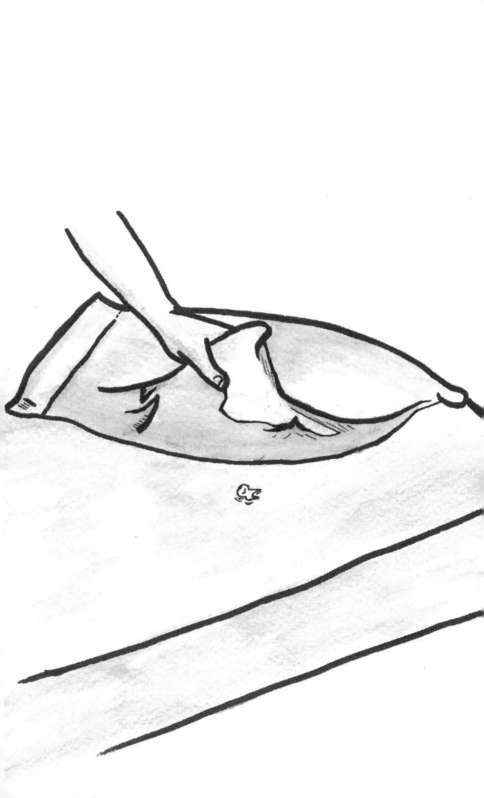

Chapter 5

Under the Pillow

-Sunday-

The next morning as soon as Annabelle awoke, full of excitement. She lifted her pillow, but to her bewilderment, her tooth was still there.

"It didn't work." She thought sadly. *"I wonder why it didn't work."*

She made her way into Marysue's room to tell her sister what had, or rather, what hadn't happened. But, Marysue was still sleeping.

Annabelle went down the hall to her parents' room to discuss the matter with them too, but, they were also still asleep.

So, Annabelle slid out a long bin from under her bed and began playing with her toys.

From down the hall she heard Mom in a frantic voice telling Dad to wake up.

"Girls, girls, quickly now! Get rinsed off in the shower and get into your church clothes or we'll be late!" She called.

Annabelle did as she was told. There was no time for breakfast. Mom gave both girls a granola bar, string cheese, and an apple. Then off they went to church.

They sat quietly next to their parents during the sermon. Marysue getting more and more anxious as the time went on.

"You'll do great dear." Her mother whispered to her reassuringly.

The pastor then stated proudly "Ladies and gentlemen, our youth has worked very hard to put together a special treat for all of us today. So will our cast please join us on stage and we will begin."

Mom gave a tight squeeze to Marysue's hand as she smiled nervously and went up front.

She did great! She remembered all of her lines. The people laughed, the people cried, and then the people clapped. They'd done it! The play was amazing.

Dad and Mom hurried backstage to help with the long process of clean up with the rest of the crew. Marysue and Annabelle helped too.

Then to celebrate the MacShannons went out to eat with friends at a fancy restaurant. Annabelle was quiet. She seemed to be lost in her own thoughts.

"Do you think she's ok?" Mom had asked Dad.

"Yeah, it's just been a very busy weekend."

When they arrived home, Mom asked Annabelle "Would you like to take a bubble bath tonight?"

Annabelle grinned from ear to ear and ran to get her bag of rubber bath toys from her closet.

Mom spent some much needed, relaxing time with both girls, brushing and braiding their hair, and talking all about their favorite parts of the play.

Even after Dad had tucked them both into their beds, mom came into their rooms to read them each a bedtime story. Annabelle listened to her mother read until she drifted off and fell fast asleep.

Chapter 6

What happened to the tooth fairy?

-Monday-

Alarms buzzed throughout the house; it was Monday morning. Time for school. Annabelle jumped out of bed got dressed and went into the bathroom to brush her... her teeth!

Before she even picked up her tooth brush, she rushed back into her bedroom and tossed her pillow out of the way eagerly. "*Wait—What!? Why?*" There, on her bed sat her tooth. "*What happened?*"

She walked back to the bathroom, shoulders slumped over, feeling defeated.

"What's wrong?" Marysue asked taking the toothpaste from her sisters hand as she walked into the bathroom.

"The Tooth Fairy, she never came." Annabelle stated sadly.

"Oh, man. I forgot about that. Did you ever find your tooth?"

"Yeah, I found it in my pocket, right where I'd left it. I put it under my pillow after we got back from Nana's..."

29

"...I put it under my pillow, after the rehearsal, but then, she didn't come! It was under there all day, and then last night she still didn't come!"

Marysue's eyes got huge. Her eyebrows were reaching up, up, and her mouth fell open. Not knowing what to say, she stuck in her toothbrush into her gaping mouth and began brushing her teeth. What could she possibly say to help her little sister at a time like this.

Annabelle left the bathroom and returned to her room. Marysue peeked into the hall, to make sure Annabelle wasn't watching, then rushed down the hall to her parents' room.

"Mom, Dad, we have a problem!" Mom and Dad looked at her confused. Marysue continued "Annabelle lost her tooth on Friday. She couldn't leave it under her pillow at Nana's 'casue she left it here by accident, in the laundry, in her pants' pocket. She's had it under her pillow ever since Saturday night, but the tooth fairy never came!"

Mom and Dad looked to each other very concerned, then they looked back to Marysue.

"Well the tooth fairy gets very busy sometimes, and uh..." Dad tried, but was at a loss for words.

"We'll talk to her honey, thank you for telling us." said mom.

At breakfast Mom and Dad both tried asking Annabelle if there was anything she wanted to talk about or share. Annabelle just shrugged her shoulders as she ate her cereal.

"Marysue told us you lost your tooth." Mom finally said.

"That's pretty exciting, which one did you loose?" Dad asked.

Annabelle opened her mouth and pointed so they could see.

"That is exciting!" Mom said. "Yeah, but the tooth fairy didn't come." whined Annabelle.

"Well, maybe she's on vacation?" Mom suggested.

"Or maybe she was kidnapped by a troll?" Then - THUMP "Ouch" Dad said. Mom had kicked him under the table, and the two exchanged looks.

"Time for the bus." Marysue said leaving the table, Annabelle followed.

"Have a good day at school you two!" Dad called. Mom walked them to the door kissing the tops of their heads and waving from the porch until they walked out of view.

On the school bus Marysue sat up front with a friend who was saving her seat. Annabelle kept walking back until she found a friendly face. She sat down next to a girl from her class, Valarie.

"Hey Annabelle, how was your weekend?"

"Busy" Annabelle said, slumping down next to her.

"Mine too, I saw your sister in the church play! She was really good."

"Yeah." Annabelle replied with a shrug.

"You ok?" She asked.

"It's just, well. I lost my tooth on Friday and the tooth fairy still hasn't come yet."

"Oh man, that stinks. Which tooth did you loose?" Valarie asked.

Annabelle pulled the tooth from her pocket and showed it to her friend.

"Oh cool!" Valarie smiled.

Hank who was sitting across from them overheard their conversation and budded in, "Oh, grow up! There's no such thing as the Tooth Fairy!"

"Don't be mean Hank!" said a girl sitting behind him.

"What?" He rolled his eyes and folded his arms in a huff.

"Don't listen to him, he's just full of nonsense." The girl said to Annabelle.

Valarie nodded in agreement "Yeah, don't listen to him Annabelle, besides, there are plenty of reasons she might not have come yet— Were you out late? My mom says when you're out late that the tooth fairy is on a very tight schedule. So, if she passed your house before you were home, she wouldn't have the time to loop back around. That happened to me once, but the Tooth Fairy came the next night."

Fred turned around on his knees, popping his head up from the seat in front of them, "Maybe your tooth had a nasty cavity in it, and that's why the tooth fairy didn't want it. That's what my dad says."

"I'm sure it wasn't that Fred!" Valarie defended "She brushes her teeth!— You do brush your teeth, right?"

"Of course I do!" Annabelle stuck her tongue out at Fred.

"FACE FRONT!" The bus driver called out, and Fred popped back down turning around to face forward in his seat.

Annabelle spent the rest of the bus ride telling Valarie all about her weekend, talking in hushed tones.

She told her how she'd left her tooth at home, and gone off to her Nana's house without it on Friday. Then she shared Nana's stories about the fairy world and the wish-coins. They had indeed gotten to bed very late on Saturday and on Sunday. It seemed reasonable that Valarie could be right. Maybe the tooth-fairy had just passed by her house already.

The rest of the school-day Annabelle pondered what may have happened to the tooth fairy. "*Did she have a busy weekend too? Had she already passed Annabelle's house each night before Annabelle got home? Was the tooth-fairy just confused, thinking that Annabelle's tooth was lost forever since she left it in her pocket that very first night? Could she actually have been kidnapped by a troll, or was she on a vacation?— Do tooth fairies really care about collecting teeth with cavities in them?*"

Chapter 7

The Payout

After school, the girls walked home together. This time, they did not race, and Marysue let Annabelle check the mail.

Inside the mailbox, there was a brown paper package, tied up with string. There were no postage markings on it, but handwritten, on the top, was Annabelle's name.

When the girls walked into the house, mom was busy folding laundry on the couch.

Annabelle went into her room and opened her mystery package. Inside the small box were several, super shiny, dimes, nickels, and even quarters. There was also a tiny, little rolled up note inside.

Annabelle,

Sorry I missed you. I came by Friday, Saturday, & Sunday, but no one was here to leave any dream dust on these coins. Please place them under your pillow for me at your earliest convenience.

Love – The Tooth Fairy.

Annabelle scratched her head. It didn't make any sense. How could she mail the tooth fairy her tooth in exchange for these coins? There wasn't even a return address. The tooth fairy didn't even ask for the tooth in her note. *"That's not how this works"* she thought.

She wondered if maybe this package might be from Nana.

Then her mother called out to her "Annabelle, Annabelle could you come in here please?"

Annabelle walked into the living room.

"I think this might be yours." Her mother said placing a hand full of coins in her hand.

"I found them, right here in your pocket, they must have been from the Tooth Fairy."

Annabelle was even more confused.

"Well, aren't you happy?" her mother asked. "The tooth fairy came after all, and that's way more money than you got last time! She must have given you some extra because she went on that vacation."

"Oh… uh, yeah. Cool." Annabelle tried to sound grateful.

The rest of their evening was uneventful, just homework and chores while mom cooked dinner and made up their lunches.

They ate dinner without Dad. He was working late.

So, only Mom had tucked them into bed.

Late that night, Annabelle heard the door. Dad was home. She heard him go into Marysue's room to say goodnight.

When he got to Annabelle's room, he knelt down to give her a hug. "Goodnight Daddy."

"Goodnight Sweetheart. Hey, look at this!" Dad released her from his embrace, pulling his hand out from under her pillow. "Coins, under your pillow! These must have been from the tooth fairy!" He exclaimed with a smile. "We'll put those in your piggy bank tomorrow."

Annabelle smiled, but she felt puzzled. She hadn't put the tooth under her pillow that night.

In fact, she'd left it in a zip lock bag that she got from her teacher that day. Her tooth was still in her backpack.

Annabelle was in a bit of a better mood the next morning as she and Marysue met in the bathroom to brush their teeth.

"I heard the Tooth Fairy finally came to our house last night." Marysue said, reaching into the medicine cabinet for her toothbrush.

"I guess so?" Annabelle replied unsure, handing over the toothpaste.

"What do you mean you guess so?" Marysue asked.

"Well, it's almost like three tooth fairies came, but I'm thinking maybe she didn't come at all… at least not the real one, it might have just been Mom, Dad, and Nana." Annabelle shrugged.

Marysue spit her toothpaste into the sink, "What makes you think that?"

Annabelle stopped brushing her teeth and hopped up onto the bathroom countertop.

"Well, yesterday after school, I got this package in the mail full of coins, and it even had a tiny rolled up note inside it from the Tooth Fairy. Then Mom said she found money in my pocket when she was doing laundry. She said that was from the Tooth Fairy. Next, when Dad came home and tucked me in, he said he found my Tooth Fairy money under my pillow too! I just don't get it."

"Well, I guess any of those could have been from the real Tooth Fairy." Marysue shrugged.

"Here's the thing though Mary, I still have my tooth!"

"What?" Marysue was genuinely surprised by that.

"Yeah. I took it with me to school yesterday, and then last night, I forgot and left it in my backpack! It wasn't even under my pillow last night." Annabelle shook her head and jumped down from the countertop.

"Wow. Hmmm, well. I don't know? Maybe mom was right, maybe she's just on vacation. Maybe if the money was from Mom and Dad, or even Nana then— well, maybe they felt like if she was on vacation, they needed to fill in for her while she's gone or something." Marysue tried.

"Maybe, but— well, if it was them just filling in then I don't think any of these coins I got are real wishing coins." Annabelle still seemed a little disappointed.

"Better do something nice with them, just incase they are." Marysue said.

Annabelle nodded as she left the bathroom. "Yeah, just in case." She agreed.

The girls finished getting ready for school, ate breakfast and said goodbye to their parents.

Annabelle got onto the school bus, her pockets full of change. She sat by Valarie, excited to tell her all that happened after school. Annabelle was eager to know what she thought of it all too.

"So, wait, you got all those coins and you still have your tooth too?" she asked.

"Yeah, wanna see?" said Annabelle, reaching into her backpack to pull out her zip lock bag, with her tooth tucked safely inside, only... only there was no tooth, the bag was full of coins! Coins and a tiny rolled up note. Eyes wide she looked in amazement toward Valarie and back to this unexpected treasure.

"What in the world!" Annabelle pulled out the note.

"No way!" Valarie exclaimed.

Dear Annabelle,

I know that your grandmother shared our story with you. So, you know just how important it is for me to get these wishes out to good dreamers. Ever since I went on vacation, I've just been so far behind. Our Waiting Wishes Wall might just topple over if I don't get these coins back into your world. I tried stopping by the over the weekend, but, it seemed no one was home. I'm on such a tight schedule you see. So, I couldn't possibly wait around. I simply could not continue waiting yet another night to get you your coins though. So, I had to drop them off. I've left your coins plus some extra, just to help me get caught up. Do help me with all the coins I've left for you, would you please? I've left you coins in several places. Please check your mail, your pockets, and under your pillow, in addition to this bag where I finally did find your lost tooth. I must thank you for always brushing so well and keeping your teeth cavity free for me so that I can always collect them from you. Please make sure these coins find good homes. Cover them with lots of dream dust for me, and spend them well.

Love, The Tooth Fairy.

P.S. Oh and I almost forgot, don't worry a bit about those mean old trolls, they haven't really bothered us in years.

The End

I can know what big words mean!

Glossary:

Anticipation: noun/ to expect something or wait for it, knowing it will happen.
"Their eyes met with anticipation." Pg. 2

Apologetically: adverb/ a way to show regret, when you show that you feel sorry.
""What happened?" Marysue asked apologetically." Pg. 2

Bewilderment: noun/ a feeling or state of shock or confusion.
"She lifted her pillow, but to her bewilderment, her tooth was still there." Pg. 25

Cacti: noun/ plural, meaning more than one cactus.
"…she gestured to her windowsill of various pots of cacti and succulents." Pg. 10

Collage(s): noun/ a collection (or group) of pictures, placed together.
"As they turned the corner, collages of family photos, new and old, lined the hallway." Pg. 6

Deliberate(ly): adverb/ to do something intentionally or, on purpose.
"…their deliberately long strides broke into a full out run." Pg. 2

Fret: verb/ to worry.
"Before Annabelle had time to fret…" Pg. 10

Heirloom: noun/ an object, usually something old, that has been passed down from your family. .
"…the touch lamp, which sat on an heirloom doily." Pg. 6

Idle(ing): verb/ to an engine running, when it's on but not moving.
"The bags and her sister were already loaded into the idling car."
Pg. 3

Ignite(d): verb/ to catch or start fire, or as a feeling, verb/ to trigger, spark, start or light up.
"…magic can be lost or it can be ignited." Pg. 12

Meticulous(ly): adverb/ very neat, or showing attention to detail.
"There were two, meticulously made, twin sized beds…" Pg. 6

Refract(ed): verb/ when light enters and then changes direction.
"Light from the setting sun, refracted off the dazzling crystal sun-catcher that dangled in the window…" Pg. 9

Shone: verb/ past tense of shine, to give out light.
"With each touch, the lamp shone brighter…" Pg. 6
"Rainbows shone in every direction." Pg. 9

Ushered: verb/ past tense of usher, to guide or to lead someone.
"…as she was being ushered down the hall towards her bedroom…"
Pg. 3
"Nana ushered the girls inside." Pg. 6

Made in the USA
Monee, IL
09 April 2023